The Earth We Love

AEK III

Outskirts Press, Inc.
http://www.outskirtspress.com

ISBN: 978-1-9772-5161-9

Edited by Erica Baran

Original Illustrations By: Nimraha © 2022. All rights reserved - used with permission.

Outskirts Press and the "OP" logo are trademarks belonging to Outskirts Press, Inc.

PRINTED IN THE UNITED STATES OF AMERICA

This book was inspired by the love
and imagination of Allen, Julia and Ian.
Their youthful and passionate view of life
will forever give me inspiration and hope!

When I was young and wild and free,
I'd go outside and climb a tree.
I would play all day without a care,
and good clean fun was everywhere.

We would hike in the hills like frontier explorers,
hunting big game, and tracking dinosaurs.
The air was so pure you could taste every smell,
and when we'd return, oh, the stories we'd tell.

When the weather got cold, it always would rain.
We would slide across the grass like a hydroplane.
We'd always end up all covered in mud,
then go home to clean up in a mountain of suds.

And the rain brought flowers all over the land,
which showed beautiful colors. It was truly quite grand.
I'd pick a whole bunch to bring home to my mother.
Then she'd make special treats for me and my brother.

After lunch, we'd all go swim in the lake.
And we'd swing from a rope and try not to break
our legs or our arms or even our neck
cause we knew if we did, we'd surely catch heck.

Then we'd walk down the road to the general store
to get root beer and candy and treats galore.
We all had a quarter, and we'd pile treats high.
It was amazing how much a quarter would buy.

As we walked back home recounting our day,
each one telling the story in their own way.
I remember thinking how great it all was
to be a kid on this planet was an incredible buzz!

But now that I'm older, I look around to see
that buildings and stores have replaced all the trees.

No longer do children run outside and play.
They just sit in their houses, all locked up away.

The hills we explored so thoroughly in our youth
Have been graded down for houses with nice tile roofs.
The great beasts that we'd tracked are all gone, it seems.
At least we still have them in our dreams.

The rain that we'd come so accustomed to seeing,
Well the fact of the matter is, it simply stopped being.
Some say it's pollution or some kind of drought,
But if you look at what we've done to this place,
there's no doubt!

The wildflowers that once covered the hills
have all been mowed under at the developer's wills.
Flowers need room to grow and expand.
Though we all loved the flowers, we needed the land.

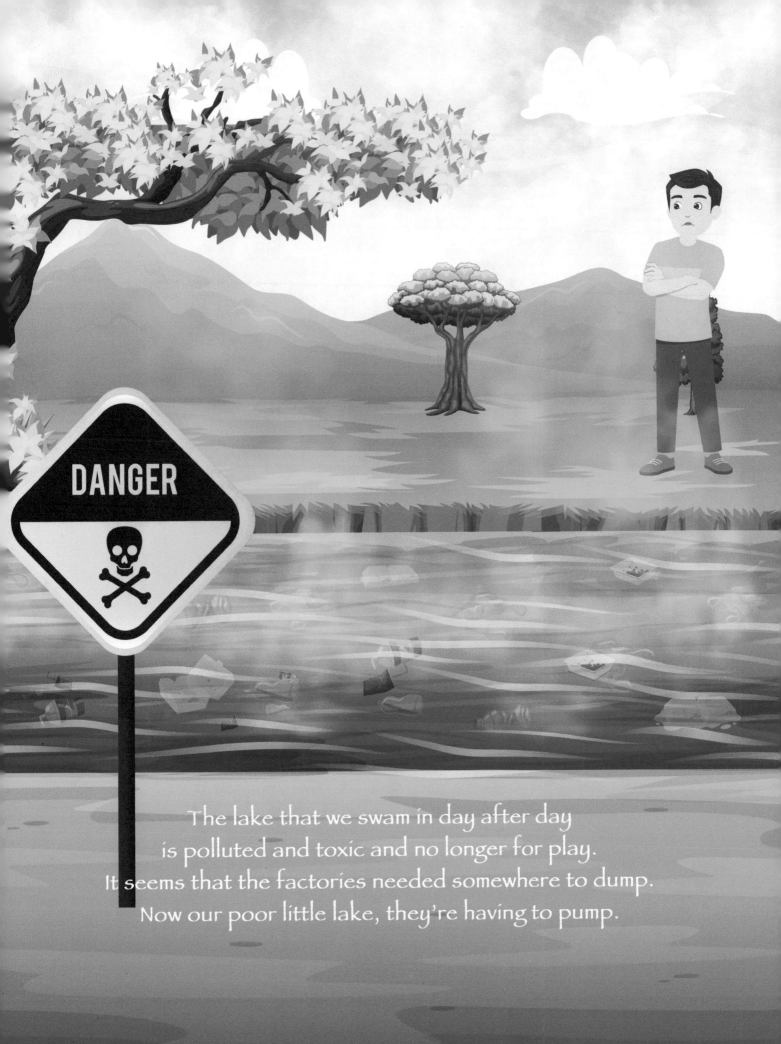

The lake that we swam in day after day
is polluted and toxic and no longer for play.
It seems that the factories needed somewhere to dump.
Now our poor little lake, they're having to pump.

SHOPPING
MALL

The general store that we used to walk to
has been replaced by a mall. Oh, what a zoo!

The quarter that once made our dreams come true
won't even buy a gumball for me and for you.

My childhood friends, well, they've all moved away.
No one has time to reminisce or just to say, "Hey."
Everyone's busy working to buy themselves things.
They've long forgotten the memories of our childhood flings.

But I think that the saddest thing of all
is that our children will never hear the call
to go out and explore with imaginations gone wild
which should be the right of every child.

But There's hope for our planet, I really think so,
For I've learned a great secret that I'd like you to know.
It's about how to live with your fellow man.
Start with love and compassion, and then work hand in hand.

For together we can make an incredible change.
We can bring it all back. I know it sounds strange.
Public awareness is a powerful thing.
If we can all see the problems, Oh, the changes we'll bring!

It's already started and growing each day,
with recycling and conservation leading the way.

And there's hybrids and
solar and much, much more.
Who knows what the future has in store?

So if you're ready to join us and make a stand,
then go to your window and scream 'cross the land:
"I'm ready for change, and I want to do good.
I'm not part of the problems in my neighborhood!"

Before you go out and get on your way,
look in the mirror, look close and say:
"Earth Day's not a day. It's a way of living!"
Then the Earth will be grateful,
bountiful, and giving!

Happy Earth Day!...Everyday!

About the Author

AEKIII (A-KEY) is a creative, passionate person that has always had a unique ability for rhyming. He loves the playful creativity of a child's imagination and creating stories that inspire that creativity. He has written over 70 childern's stories and hopes to begin publishing them very soon.